Abhirup Dhar is a Kolkata-born bestselling author. His books include *Once Again... With Love!* and *Stories Are Magical* after which he delved into horror with *Hold That Breath (1 and 2), Hauntings* and *The Belvoirbrooke Haunting* which were very well-received, with *Hauntings* being an Amazon bestseller for months from the very first day of its release. A name to be reckoned with in the genre of horror writing in India, one of his most famous projects, *Ghost Hunter: Gaurav Tiwari,* was phenomenally received, topped the Amazon charts, and has been acquired for a screen adaptation. Abhirup is also a screenwriter, working with esteemed people from the Indian film industry.

Praise for Abhirup Dhar

"There are very few writers who write horror and write it well. Abhirup Dhar is one of them. I wish him all the best on his next book that comes after his already successful horror outing."

—Vikram Bhatt, Filmmaker

"Abhirup Dhar has put Indian horror in the limelight with his books which have broken through the clutter. Rarely has the genre reached out so well."

—Jay K, Film director

"Dhar is the biggest Indian horror writer in the country and one of the most renowned authors who keeps us holding our breath!"

—*Mid-Day*

"With his spooky and relatable brand of horror, Abhirup Dhar has reinvented the genre."

—Vishal Mahadkar, Film director

"Abhirup Dhar's unique voice puts a fresh spin on a genre as old as time. Wonderfully creepy stories with an international flavour. Dig in, horror fans!"

—Internationally acclaimed, award-winning horror writer Ken Stark on Dhar's *Hold That Breath*

"This is modern-day literature at its best, gripping you from the word go with all the elements of entertainment."

—*Daily Hunt*

KARMA

ABHIRUP DHAR

Om Books International

First published in 2024 by

Om Books International

Corporate & Editorial Office
A-12, Sector 64, Noida 201 301
Uttar Pradesh, India
Phone: +91 120 477 4100
Email: editorial@ombooks.com
Website: www.ombooksinternational.com

Sales Office
107, Ansari Road, Darya Ganj,
New Delhi 110 002, India
Phone: +91 11 4000 9000
Email: sales@ombooks.com
Website: www.ombooks.com

ISBN: 978-81-19750-52-8

Printed in India

10 9 8 7 6 5 4 3 2 1

To my readers, for your immense support,
My parents, whose struggles are remembered,
Chandrani, my confidante, my best friend, my love,
Kaira, my daughter, the light of my life,
Oliver, my fur baby

To the past that has shaped me,
the present that nurtures me,
the future that awaits me

PROLOGUE

1985

Ricky was alone at his home in Darjeeling. His mother, Anuradha, was in Calcutta to attend a family wedding. It was the final month of school and her six-year-old had to prepare for his exams. So, it was decided Ricky would stay home with his father, Arnab. But a few days later, Arnab was called to work and asked to leave for Siliguri. Unfortunately, Ricky was sick and had a high fever, and his father had to leave him under the care of a nurse, who was to attend to him till he was back the next day.

The evening his father left, alone and free from the burden of studying, Ricky was more than willing to slip under the warm blanket after an early dinner. The bedroom was large and cosy, with big glass windows and a main door connected to the common dining room. The whole house was huge and stood in a secluded spot, away from the town and its bustle, in the lap of nature;

a serene, quiet place. His eyelids felt heavy, and he was quick to doze off to sleep. The ticking clock was the only thing piercing the silence of the night until Ricky suddenly woke up, loudly gasping for breath. His hands hurriedly tried to remove whatever he felt weighing on his chest but found nothing. He struggled to breathe for a few more minutes and blamed his sickness for what he thought was a bad dream. He opened the windows and took deep breaths; the cold air eased him. He observed the full moon and its light flooding the verandah outside. It was beautiful and he started to calm down. There was no one around. Just him alone, the illuminated verandah, and the leaves on the trees swaying in the breeze, which could as well be taking the shape and sound of strong winds in some time. He was now wide awake, enjoying the night and humming a song to himself. Just then his peace was disturbed by a sound. The noise was coming from his room, he was sure. Ricky looked around and felt a sudden coldness grip him which had nothing to do with the chill breeze coming in through the window.

"Is anyone here? Sister?" he called for the nurse. Maybe it was she, he thought. But there was no reply.

He walked barefoot on the cold floor up to the main door and tried to open it. The door didn't budge. He then tried to switch on the light but there was no electricity.

Ricky stood there shivering from the cold and the eeriness of the night. Then, he heard the noise again. It was clearer this time. But he still had to strain his ears to understand it. It was the voice of a man.

"Who..." Ricky stuttered, moving back a few steps.

The door of his room opened by itself, and he could now hear the grand piano playing in the living room. Taking unsure steps, Ricky slowly walked to the living room and peeked inside. There he saw a woman sitting at the piano. She was wearing a long, flowing dress. Her back was turned to Ricky so he couldn't see her face. It couldn't be the nurse. He was puzzled. With one push, he opened the door. Suddenly the lady was no longer there. Ricky was confused and terrified. He had witnessed a woman vanish into thin air in the blink of an eye. The air felt heavy and still. His heart was racing, and even in the cold, he felt his body sweating.

Ricky thought it was best to go to his room when he heard the noise again. This time he could tell the voice was trying to tell him something. It was now coming from the living room as if it had followed him there.

There was a large antique mirror kept there. It was given to the previous owner as a gift, and as per him, dated back to the 1850s. The owner had never lived in the house, however. He lived abroad and would come to Darjeeling once every three to four years but even when he was in the town, he would put up in a hotel. The house was one of the many he owned as investments until he decided to sell it to Ricky's parents.

"Where is the nurse?" Ricky mumbled to himself. In the dark, he felt for the walls to reach for the drawers and searched for a torch.

Just then, he heard the piano play again. Ricky flashed the light towards it. The music stopped.

Am I hallucinating? Maybe it's just a mouse messing with the piano? He tried to console himself and began walking back to the door. And then it started to play again. A startled Ricky looked back. This time, it didn't stop.

A tune most hauntingly melodious disrupted the silence. He was unsettled by it. It was as if it wanted to convey something to him. Now this could not be a hallucination, a stunned Ricky admitted to himself.

He stood there frozen, flashing his torchlight at the piano where he could see no one, yet the piano continued playing.

"Who… Who is it?" he stuttered.

"Who is it?" He asked again, this time louder. Ricky tried hard to muster all his courage, and it worked. The music stopped.

Now there was a noise, hurried whispers. He strained his ears to listen. *No, it still doesn't make sense.*

"What is it?" he cried.

"What are you trying to tell me?" he yelled.

One of the large windows opened and brought inside a gust of wind. Then, the noise grew louder too. He could hear it better now; a man and a woman were in a heated argument.

The piano played again. The arguments continued along with its distant strains. The noise gradually began to get louder and louder. The glass windows vibrated; the walls seemed to shudder. He felt his head was going to burst. He couldn't bear it and shut his ears with his hands to drown out the noise.

"No!" he screamed. And in a split second, all was quiet again.

Ricky sat down on a chair, dreading to move even an inch. He knew he should've run but in the uncanny silence, he was engulfed by fear that made him too numb to make a move.

"Ricky…" a voice whispered in his ears. He felt hot breath on his ears, and then he heard a woman giggle.

"If I die before you, I'll come back and haunt you!" Her piercing voice echoed in the room.

Ricky cried out loud and just as he turned to run towards the door, he heard the man speak. He looked back closely. The voices seemed to be coming from the mirror kept near the piano.

"Just tell me the truth! Please…" The man's scream was followed by a thud, as if someone had fallen hard on the ground.

Ricky looked closely again. He could see shadows moving in the mirror. He saw a man's silhouette become clearer. "No… No…" He wept.

"Who are you?" Ricky cried.

His body was paralysed by a force unknown. He struggled to move and screamed the question at the voices he could hear.

Ricky then saw the man call out from inside the mirror; his voice choking, as if he was suffocating and life was slowly and painfully slipping out of his body…

"What is this?" the young and frightened Ricky cried, biting his tongue once to check if he was in the middle of a nightmare. It hurt. He was terrified. This was real.

"What do you want to say?" he cried again.

And then, he heard the man…

"D-E-A-T-H," he said and gasped for air one last time.

The next moment, there was no one in the mirror.

"Ricky *baba*, are you okay?" The nurse was at the door flashing a torch in his face.

CHAPTER ONE

Dark, grey clouds surrounded the sky, like a predator encircling its prey. A startling low rumble rang loud in the cool fall air. Drops of rain fell on the ground, at first gently and then with increasing vigour, as the drizzle turned into a barrage. While a dense, earthy, sweet smell enveloped everything in its soft embrace, the road and streets of the city of Darjeeling were submerged in muddy waters. What had begun as a drizzle moments before turned into a torrential downpour, forewarning a harsher storm.

Amid this, Karma and Sakshi were stuck in their house. All networks were dead; they couldn't use the landline or their phones. The electricity supply was cut before it even began to rain and the house was covered in darkness. The storm was gaining momentum, and they couldn't leave their home. But they had to find help somehow. It wasn't about the fast-approaching storm. It was about the house they lived in, where they were stranded. For some time, there had been signs that something was gravely wrong. Strange things were happening in the house, inexplicable things. All of it had started from that particular morning, and their home had not felt the same ever since...

It was raining that day too. The sound of loud footsteps had woken Karma up that morning. He heard the main door of the house open and shut and there was the noise of people whispering among themselves—prominently the voice of a man and a woman. Throughout that day, he could hear strange sounds. Initially what Karma had dismissed as concoctions of his sleepy brain grew into disruptions that were heard at other times; the laughter of a little boy, footsteps in the empty living room, or brief piano notes playing on their own. Things were starting to get lost too. Sakshi would wake up and find her things not where she had placed them. They couldn't both be imagining things? Were they going mad? Karma and Sakshi found it hard to make sense of things. And it was becoming increasingly difficult to live in the house.

One night, Karma stood in front of the mirror in his room when he saw the reflection of a lady, her face obscured by a hazy blur that refused to sharpen into focus. He heard a terrifying scream as the blurry mass split open, revealing a gaping void where her mouth should have been.

"Sak..." His voice choked in fear as the woman disappeared in a flash.

Just then, the door of the room flung open. Karma stood there frozen for a while.

"What's going on, Karma?" Sakshi woke up from sleep. He kept from her what he had just witnessed. He held her hands and tried to comfort her. "Everything is okay. I thought I saw something but it was nothing. Don't worry. Go back to sleep," he told her and tucked her in. Perhaps this is how it is when people are in love—it becomes their nature to summon strength for their loved ones even when they feel weak.

The next afternoon, Karma heard the piano playing in the living room.

"Sakshi..." he called for her but there was no response.

It couldn't be her. She knew how to play the piano well. This sounded more like a disturbance—someone playing the keys as a trick for fun or attention.

Karma walked to the living room and found a little boy seated on the stool facing the grand piano, clearly in some mood for mischief.

"Could it be the neighbour's son?" Karma mumbled and thought it over. Why would the little boy come to their house during the storm and importantly, how would he get in without anyone opening the door? They were unable to go out themselves. Something was wrong with the door. It wouldn't open.

"Someone must have locked it from outside... the kids from Thapa's house perhaps?" Sakshi said.

"The door seems to be stuck... the rain might have caused the wood to swell or something..." Karma suggested.

Confused, Karma strode across the living room to talk to the boy. But as his hands reached to touch his shoulders, the boy disappeared into thin air!

"What happened?" Sakshi came rushing to where her husband stood.

Karma shivered as he hugged Sakshi. He was beginning to feel scared. Even if they kept pretending things were fine, he knew none of this was normal. There was an eerie silence in the living room and suddenly, they both heard the sound of footsteps around them. They couldn't see anyone but could feel the presence of someone else in the room.

2016

It was going to be a hectic month for Karma Dutta. Being the senior professor, he had to conceptualise many sessions for the inter-collegiate seminar being held in his college. He would also have to contribute to a few of these sessions as a speaker and moderator. Karma Dutta was well-known in Darjeeling not just as a highly respected teacher but also as a prolific writer. He had authored several books on parapsychology, a subject he devoted all his free time to. Karma had lived in the hills as a child, and it was only a few years ago that he had moved here again and took up the job of a junior professor. Karma excelled well in the subject he taught, and his books were quite popular among experts and enthusiasts alike. In no time, he emerged as one of the most distinguished professors. But he chose to maintain a low profile. His books travelled far while he was rarely ever seen giving an interview. It wasn't that he was insecure or lacked esteem. He was just reserved in life. That's the way he had always been. It suited him. He only needed two things after a long day of work—time and silence to concentrate on his writing. At thirty-seven, he was doing well for himself. Success for him was not about money. After a string of several nonfiction books, he was working on the most important book of his writing career; with this one, he was attempting to understand the afterlife, something he had become curious about as a child after losing his parents.

Many colleges from various parts of the country were invited for the inter-collegiate seminar at Mount Hermon College, Darjeeling. This was a first for the hill station which was generally very popular among tourists. Everyone was very excited. The event was being sponsored by some of the biggest names in Darjeeling and they all expected a big boost in tourism too, which was the main source of income for so many people. The news coverage would be an icing on the cake and a rather neglected part of the country would be in the limelight for the right reason—a fun event on education where many teachers and students from across the country were participating. Karma knew the event was going to be a hit!

Sakshi Basu, a college student from Kolkata, one of the many invitees to the event, was in Darjeeling for the first time and had already fallen in love with the city and the freedom she could experience here for the first time. The twenty-five-year-old carefree girl had been looking forward to something else too—meeting Dr Karma Dutta. She had been an avid reader of his books and an earnest fan. She was not going to hesitate to approach him and so on the first day of the seminar, during the break between the sessions, Sakshi decided to speak to him.

"Big fan!" she said and her eyes twinkled as she requested him for an autograph on his latest book which she had been carrying with her.

"I'm… humbled." A shy Karma smiled while signing on it.

"Can I ask you a question? Your books are everywhere, read by so many people, yet we barely see you anywhere. Why do you escape the crowd?" Sakshi asked.

Taken aback by her directness, Karma took a few seconds to compose himself. "I'm just not comfortable giving interviews and attending all these events. One can't be themselves there. It feels pretentious at times and... I can't be that!" he answered.

"Fair enough. And why has your writing suddenly taken a creative turn?"

"What do you mean?" Karma asked, a little embarrassed.

"Well, you seem to be adding a lot of drama to your books."

"It's what the publishers want. I am told that is how my books will sell more. That's what keeps the reader engaged. And I am, of course, writing for the readers and not just for myself."

"But where is the joy then?"

"Excuse me?"

"Hadn't you once said that you write for the sheer joy of writing and that though you're exploring the paranormal, you are still writing from the heart? I also remember you had expressed your dislike for commercialisation. You don't believe in all that anymore, huh?"

Karma was left stunned for a few seconds.

"The autograph..." Sakshi broke the spell.

"Ah, yes... hmm... what's your name?"

"Sakshi."

Karma wrote her name with a short message and handed the signed book to her.

"Thanks," he told her.

"I should be saying that…" Sakshi smiled as she looked at the autograph.

"No. Thanks, Sakshi. Thanks for speaking to the writer in me," he said to her and shook her hand.

"Could I take you out for a coffee one of these days?" Sakshi posed the question very casually. Karma looked at her for a moment. She looked like she feared nothing. Wearing trendy casuals, she was diametrically opposite to Karma, who came off as restrained and guarded in his formals. He hadn't met anyone like her. He hardly had any friends while growing up, and now was so busy shaping the prospective careers of his students that he had time for nothing else. Not that he felt any kind of a void either. He never really thought about matters of love and the heart. There had been women who were interested in him, mostly fellow teachers, but he never responded to their advances. Some took his reticence for rudeness. But it was different with Sakshi. He couldn't explain what force made him agree, but he said yes to the date.

Their first official meeting happened a day later, on Saturday, when the program involving Karma was wrapped up within the first half of the day. The ten-day seminar would continue into the next week as well which meant, the invitees would have to stay in Darjeeling for another weekend. They met at Glenary's, a famous old heritage restaurant, for dinner and bonded well over food, drinks and conversation. They shared mutual feelings for a few things but were largely very different from each other. While Karma was an introvert, Sakshi was his antithesis—a spirited, outgoing, happy-go-lucky charmer. Not that Karma didn't have his charms, he just exhibited them quietly.

It was evident that they enjoyed being around each other. They met every day after the event, and Karma made it a point to drop her at the hotel after their dates, before heading back home, reaching late, barely finding any time to read or write. This was unlike him. The habits of his daily life were transforming and he couldn't care less. Despite the difference in their age, they still were in sync. Apart from going out to eat, they also visited a few tourist attractions when they could afford to leave the college early. They loved the smell and sight of orchids at the Rock Garden. On some days, they would also go together to see the sunrise from Tiger Hill. With each passing day, they started to know each other better. And they had one peculiar interest in common—their love for haunted places. For Karma, the fascination owed itself to his books and his past experiences. During his time in Darjeeling, he had made it a point to visit all the places infamous for being haunted. One of his books was based on the research he did here. This could have also been one of the reasons why Sakshi was curious about such locations in Darjeeling. It was her favourite among all his books. Karma and Sakshi were thrilled to make these visits. Karma found himself talking a lot more than he ever did. Sakshi was impressed by his maturity. It never bothered them that Karma was twelve years older than her. They liked each other and were happy to spend time together; nothing else mattered.

At night, they spent hours talking to each other on the phone, much to the dismay of Sakshi's roommate at the hotel.

"I'll have to whisper… okay?" Sakshi asked.

Karma chuckled. "Yes. It's cute. Here, I'll whisper too. Even the ghosts won't hear us."

She laughed. "So, you haven't told me about your family. All I know is that you stay here alone."

He was quiet, and then to deflect answering he said, "Why don't you tell me about yours."

"Nothing worth mentioning…"

"Why?"

"It's not new or uncommon...just one dysfunctional family. My father owns a chain of restaurants and is filthy rich. But he was a big failure in his personal life. So was my mother—another failure. They divorced a few years ago and both remarried. I live with my father."

"I am sure it wasn't easy growing up through the mess. But at least you still have parents, Sakshi. Good or bad, you know they are alive. I lost my parents when I was very young."

"I didn't know this. I'm so sorry."

"Never mind. It's been years now. It feels like a distant nightmare."

"Let's talk about something else…"

"Like?"

"Anything. I want to keep hearing you talk."

"I like listening to you too…"

"Aha! Tell me about your ex-girlfriends?" Sakshi asked mischievously.

Karma was silent for a few seconds. Sakshi could sense that he didn't like to reveal the private details of his life.

"I had one, years ago, back in college. Things didn't work out between us and she is married now. You?"

"What? Any girlfriends?" Sakshi giggled. "I was seeing someone not long ago. He was more of a crush!"

"Hmm."

"Anyway, before I sleep, Karma, word of advice—you need to loosen up a bit."

"Well, Sakshi. How does one do that?"

"Maybe you can start by wearing less formal clothes!" Sakshi teased him.

"Why? What's wrong with my clothes?"

"Nothing. Just that you don't need to wear formals all the time, you know."

"But…"

"Okay, now I go. I don't want my roommate to wake up annoyed. See you."

The next morning, Karma was a differently dressed man. He turned heads and not just because he looked good. Nobody in the institute had seen him wear anything but his usual attire—a light-coloured shirt, dark trousers, and a grey blazer. On special days he would throw in a tie. His hair was always neatly combed with not a strand out of place. But today was different. He wore a bright red check shirt tucked well in a pair of blue jeans; his slightly messy hair complementing his casual manner of dressing. He seemed to be moving freely, like he had no burdens on his shoulders. There was a change in the way he walked too. He looked more at ease.

When Sakshi saw the changed man during the break, she was happily surprised.

"Look at you!" She whistled.

He smiled at her. What they felt on seeing each other was new and intense, and there was no stopping it. They were beginning to fall for each other.

CHAPTER TWO

standing still, staring into the large antique mirror with empty eyes.

"What happened, Ricky *baba*?" the nurse asked, but he wouldn't answer. After trying to probe him to say something, she let him go to his room. The next morning, his father was back and was told by the nurse about what had transpired the night before.

"I had woken up to get some water and thought I would check on Ricky *baba*. But he wasn't in his room."

"What were you doing in the living room, Ricky?" Arnab asked his son. But he said nothing. Arnab could understand that something was wrong with him; maybe he had sleepwalked out of his room or had a nightmare. Whatever it was, Ricky was deeply affected by it. He hugged Ricky and tried to comfort him. Anuradha had also rushed back home after Arnab had told her about what had happened. They both could see something had changed in Ricky. And as they were to find out soon, something had changed in the house too.

It started with strange noises which were often heard in the house. Sometimes there were sounds of footsteps; sometimes there were whispers. There were times when they could hear a man and a woman weeping. They could also feel eyes on them, as if they were being watched.

A few days later, Ricky was lazily playing the keys of the grand piano in the living room when he heard a voice call for him. Startled, he turned around but found nobody there. "I heard a voice, Mom. It was a man..." he told his mother solemnly. While Anuradha and Arnab were convinced of the strange occurrences in the house, they didn't want to admit to it and alarm Ricky. But it wasn't that they were ignoring it either. They were waiting to understand what trouble was lurking in the house and figure a way out of it.

"Should we consider moving back, Arnab?" Anuradha asked her husband.

"I have invested all my savings into this house and the business here, Anu. You know that. Let's... let's just do the best we can. Perhaps, the *vaastu* wasn't good here. We'll do something about this. We'll get it fixed. We'll figure something out," he replied.

After the incident, Anuradha had insisted they move the vintage mirror to their bedroom. Her superstitions led her to believe it was bad practice to keep it in the living room. Besides she found it complemented their room better. That night, she was combing her hair, seated in front of that mirror when she suddenly screamed. "Arnab!" she called her husband who had just gone to bed. "There was... a man..." she stuttered.

"Arnab..." Anuradha hugged her husband and began crying.

"Are you sure, Anu? You've been stressed about the house and Ricky. Maybe the distress is making you imagine things? Just think it over..."

"No... No... Arnab..." she kept crying.

"Anu, I'll fix everything, I promise. Come, let's try to get some sleep." Arnab kissed her forehead and tried to console her.

But Anuradha was sure about what she saw. It couldn't just be her imagination.

The apparition was warped and distorted. His features were ghoulish, his eyes hollow and soulless, glaring at Anuradha with hostility. Then the reflection had shifted, morphing into something altogether more sinister. The man's image contorted and twisted, his face melting and reforming into a ghastly visage of horror. And then it had vanished. Anuradha had sat there frozen in fear as the horror unfolded in front of her eyes, a nightmare she had seen with her eyes wide open.

That same night, a little past twelve, Ricky woke up thirsty. He switched on the dim table lamp and checked the jug for water but found it empty, so he got out of bed and walked to the kitchen to drink some water. While going back to his room, he heard a noise. At first, he felt someone's steps behind him. Ricky strained his ears to listen. The footsteps could be heard from the living room. Loud, heavy steps, like someone was dragging their feet on the floor.

It was dark in the hallways and the only dim light came from his bedroom, whose door he had left open.

Ricky stood there still, afraid of making a sound and attracting the attention of whoever was moving in the living room. But he let his eyes look around and, in the darkness he spotted a man walking…

The sound of his footsteps echoed through the house. His movements were slow and disjointed, and with each weary step, he traced the same path, pacing endlessly in the middle of the living room.

2016

On the day the sessions were going to commence a little late, Karma and Sakshi decided to explore the outskirts of the city. They had already visited the major tourist attractions in town. They had been making the most of it in the early mornings or late evenings. For this excursion, Karma had asked her to be ready by 6 a.m.

And there she was that morning, looking beautiful as ever. Karma had only seen her wearing smart casuals so far and she preferred to keep it simple; only a dark shade of red lipstick and a perfume which complemented her allure. And that day too she was dressed plainly—a short *kurti* over a pair of old, worn-out jeans. Her hair was held in a bun like she had hurriedly tied it without a care. Karma looked at her and found in her the most beautiful woman he had ever seen. A smile escaped his lips as he met her eyes that cold morning.

"Hi." Sakshi greeted him with a dazzling smile. *What is this feeling?* he thought sheepishly. Karma had never felt like this before. Sakshi made him go weak in his knees.

"What… Why are you smiling?" Sakshi asked though she could sense why.

"Nothing. Nothing. Let's go." He opened the door of the car for Sakshi.

Inside the car, they looked at each other for a few seconds. Karma didn't want the moment to pass. He'd never been as happy as he felt now.

"So… Where are you taking me?" Sakshi broke the silence.

"Ah, we have a few days till the fest is over. And I'd like to take you to a few places around the town now. Okay?" Karma turned the ignition key.

It took them a little over thirty minutes to reach Lepchajagat, a small village in the wilderness, not very far away from the town. The night before, after leaving Sakshi at the hotel, Karma had made it a point to pack some ham and cheese sandwiches and bacon.

"We have enough food... in case you get hungry," he told Sakshi.

"Thanks. What would I do without you!" Sakshi reached for the packet and took out a sandwich.

Soon, they were away from the town, traversing the hilly terrain that weaved like a silver thread through the green hills, undulating, leading into the horizon.

Sakshi opened all the windows of the car and felt the cold breeze. It was a lovely morning. To think that she was with Karma and now knew him so well; that he was with her, probably feeling the same way she felt for him—that realisation for her was blissful.

A few minutes later, they reached a deserted hamlet.

"This?" Sakshi looked around. Lines and lines of trees surrounded them and there was not a single person in sight.

"Yes. This," Karma said.

"Let me park my car here and then we can walk around," he added.

"Not a bad idea."

Karma locked the car and caught up with Sakshi who had walked a few steps ahead.

"Have you been here before?" Sakshi looked at Karma.

"Long ago. I was here for a long time," Karma told her.

"I see. Beautiful."

"You are." Karma thought he thought it. But he had uttered the words for Sakshi to hear.

"Hmm?" She smiled.

"Nothing."

Why am I behaving like a lovestruck teenager? he thought and shook his head, embarrassed.

"You know, Karma, from your books, I had assumed you to be a very serious guy."

"But I am, no?"

"Not entirely. A part of you is still a child at heart." Sakshi stopped and took a good look at Karma.

They were all alone amid the hilly forest area. It was a beautiful day. They could hear the leaves swaying in the breeze in the serene silence. Time seemed to have come to a standstill. It was a place away from the world allowing them to admit to themselves what was in their hearts. They knew they had feelings for each other but waited for the other to confess it first.

"I was thinking…" Karma initiated.

"I like you," Sakshi said.

Karma was taken aback. "I wanted to…" He smiled shyly at her, unable to complete his sentence. Sakshi walked up to Karma and held him, and he kissed her.

In that kiss was the sweetness of passion, a million things of beauty condensed into a moment. It was perfect. As if, they had come to the world for this moment alone. Nothing else mattered.

The wind roared outside the house. Karma looked at the clock which was stuck at 1:10. Several hours had passed since it had stopped working. *Or days?* he thought. The storm outside had receded for some time or so it seemed to Karma and Sakshi. They could hear the wind accompanied by the rustling trees as their limbs strained against the onslaught.

"We need to run away from here." With every word, Karma revealed his desperation to escape the jinxed house.

"But… the door…" Sakshi reminded him that they had been trapped inside the house.

"I'll try again." Karma walked up to the main door of the house and saw it open on its own. He looked in astonishment and confusion at Sakshi, who mirrored his reaction.

The door swung against the wall, banging loudly while the howling wind entered the house.

"Come…" Karma extended his hand for Sakshi to hold it.

Then the rain began to pour down, heavily, without mercy, so thick that they couldn't see a yard ahead.

"We just need to run… Okay?" Karma instructed Sakshi. This was the only way they could move away from the house and get some help.

So, they ran with all the strength they could muster while the rain pattered just as strongly, making each step a test of endurance. Both Karma and Sakshi ran on an empty road through the forest area. They could see nothing and hear nothing.

"We have to… We have to get somewhere… anywhere!" Karma reiterated as they continued running.

"How long has it been?" Sakshi stopped and asked.

"How long what?"

"Us… running. What else? What else, Karma? Can you recall when we left the house? How long have we been running for and where are we headed for God's sake!"

Karma went closer to Sakshi and hugged her.

"You are scared, Sakshi. So am I."

"Will we always be stuck here, Karma?" she whispered fearfully. "Strange things have been happening since we came here. None of it makes sense. Tell me if you can recall when we left the house."

"No… No… The house is playing games with us… We have to run…"

"But where?"

"Anywhere!" Karma screamed and burst into tears.

"The house won't let us go anywhere, Karma. Can't you see it?" Sakshi screamed back.

"Don't say that… Don't say that…" Karma kicked the ground hard and moved closer to Sakshi to hug her. But a dense fog started to envelop them. The next moment they could barely see each other.

"Karma…" Sakshi whispered, trying to find Karma's hand to hold in the fog. All of a sudden, the wind had stopped howling.

"Karma…" she whispered again and brought his hand closer to herself.

But she couldn't reach his body. He wasn't there. Instead, she felt thick warm liquid cover her fingers. Sakshi let out a scream as she threw Karma's severed hand away, fresh blood dripping from it onto the ground.

"Karma…" she cried loudly and ran without knowing where she was going. Her head was numb, she could hear nothing. Only the sound of her footsteps followed her.

And then, just like that, she found herself back inside the house. And there he was. "Karma…" she looked at him in great surprise. "Where the hell did you go?" she screamed at him.

"I was here, Sakshi," he replied solemnly.

"What are you saying?" She moved away from him. "We ran… ran away from this damned house… don't you remember?" she cried.

"That was a few days ago, Sakshi. It was a futile attempt. We managed to open the main door and run… and soon we were surrounded by a dense fog..."

"Yes… Yes… That happened today… That happened just now!"

"No. I was here. I have been here for a while."

"And where was I?"

"You said you were going to the basement…"

"No, Karma. No. Why won't you believe me?"

"I do, Sakshi. This house… it's messing with our heads..." he whispered softly as Sakshi held his hands tightly. "Look… Sak…" Karma looked at the clock in the room again. The clock was working now, but it was ticking backwards.

The ticking became an otherworldly cacophony, each tick resounding with a dissonance that sent chills down their spines. Whispers, ethereal and tormented, intertwined with the ticking, created an unholy chorus. Just then, they heard the piano being played in the living room. Karma and Sakshi rushed to the room which was again empty, with only the sound of the piano echoing within its walls. But it wasn't being played by any amateur now. This was a piece that only a learned hand could play.

"Who is here?" Karma shouted.

The piano stopped playing.

Karma and Sakshi stood there looking at it.

The next moment, music filled the room again, playing a melancholic melody. There was no visible player, yet the keys were pressed with an otherworldly grace. The candles flickered, creating a mesmerizing interplay of light and darkness. Karma and Sakshi stood stupefied and couldn't utter a word. They held each other tightly as the tragic tune reached its crescendo.

Then lightning struck and flooded the interiors of the dark house with intermittent flashes of light. The tune got more intense... and before it could reach its finale it abruptly stopped.

"Who is here?" Karma's voice broke the silence.

"Answer us!" Sakshi said.

"Answer us!" they shouted together.

Both stood still as they watched the sitting stool near the piano move back by itself. Then they heard someone walk up to the main door.

"Who are you?" Karma and Sakshi screamed.

They heard a loud thud as if someone had been pushed hard towards a wall. Someone wept. But they could see nobody!

Sakshi walked to one side of the living room and lit a candle.

"Maa..." she heard a little boy's voice from behind and someone blew out the candle.

Karma and Sakshi heard footsteps run from one end of the living room to the other.

The living room was shrouded in darkness, illuminated only by the dim moonlight seeping through the dusty windows where the curtains were drawn. Small mirrors adorned the walls, reflecting eerie images of the empty room. A faint mist seemed to swirl in the glass, distorting the reflections. Suddenly, the silence was shattered by the faint sound of giggling. A small boy's laughter echoed through the room, but no one was there.

The mirror on the wall across the piano flickered, reflecting the image of the little boy running in the room. He was dressed in a yellow raincoat with a cap on his head. Karma and Sakshi stood in front of it. They could see his ghostly visage. He was giggling.

The little boy stopped suddenly. He turned towards Karma and Sakshi, but his face was not visible.

"Maa, help me!" He sobbed.

Sakshi looked clueless as the boy continued crying. Karma reached out to touch the mirror, but his hand passed through the glass as if it was water! And the boy was gone.

Karma stepped back looking pale and frightened. Just then, there was the boy's laughter again. The laughter grew louder, echoing through the room. Karma spun around, searching for the little boy's reflection in the large mirror. Suddenly, its surface began to shake violently. Karma stumbled backwards; his eyes wide with terror.

"Maa, please… please help me!" the little boy's voice echoed.

Karma rushed towards the mirror again, desperation etched on his face. He pressed his hands against the glass, feeling a strange energy pulsating beneath his fingertips. As he stared into the mirror, his reflection began to distort. The room spun around him, and he felt himself being pulled into the darkness.

Just then there was a knock on the main door. Though terrified and uneasy, Karma walked towards it and peeped through the eyehole.

The same boy stood outside. He wore a bright yellow raincoat, his face partially covered by its cap.

"Who… Who are you? What are you doing here at this hour?" Karma managed to utter the words.

"Maa, I'm home!" the little boy cried as if he couldn't hear Karma.

"Your mom… your mom isn't here," Karma said, this time in a lower voice.

"Please open the door, maa," the boy cried harder.

Karma looked at Sakshi baffled. Sakshi's face had a blank expression but she went ahead and peeped through the eyehole too.

"There is nobody here, Karma…"

A shocked Karma saw through the door again and found nobody outside, only the pouring rain that seemed to herald devastation and ruin, a sense of which he could also feel within him.

CHAPTER THREE

2016

Karma and Sakshi walked on the road through the forest area. It took them a few minutes to reach the place where Karma wanted to take her.

"This is it." He smiled as they reached a house.

It was a big single-storey house built into a sloping roof with dormer windows, surrounded by wide verandas. There was a small lawn too.

It was an old house but so beautiful that Sakshi kept staring at it for almost a minute till she could react.

"What a beautiful house..." she said in awe.

"This is my dream house," Karma told her, as if revealing to her a big secret.

There was a 'For Sale' board on the gate. Karma threw it away, took out a key from his pocket and opened the lock on the main door. They walked around its huge garden. "You know I lived in Darjeeling for a few years as a child, right?"

"Yes. You've mentioned it."

"I lived in this house."

"Wow!"

"Yes. This place. I have some very fond memories of living here."

Sakshi smiled and kissed Karma's cheek. "That's sweet."

"Ah, is it? But really, I've got a new meaning to life now that you are with me, Sakshi. I would never want to lose you..." He kissed her.

"I've lost so many people in my life that I can't trust anything good that happens to me. I'm scared of losing it all... I'll always be scared of losing you..."

"Even if I die before you, I'll come back to haunt you! Don't worry!" She giggled and kissed him.

Karma's eyes sparkled with joy. "I am glad I get to share this moment with you. Now this house is mine! It's a dream come true." He stood up unable to hold back his excitement.

"I am so happy for you, Karma."

They walked back to where the car was parked. They had a long conversation before driving back to the town.

The next day was the last day of the intercollegiate fest, which was a grand success. Dr Karma Dutta was acknowledged for putting up a great show as he had headed the team responsible for much of the organisation and coordination. But all he could think of was Sakshi. It would be the last day he could take her out.

"You will come back, right?" Karma held her hand and placed it near his heart. He kissed her fingers one by one.

It was late at night when they decided to drive outside the town again. Karma parked the car in a quiet place.

The sky was clear and they could see an abundance of glittering stars.

They sat in the backseat of the car with a can of chilled beer each, celebrating the last day of being together until Sakshi, keeping her promise, would return.

As his hands moved over her skin, her mind was trapped by desire's heady demands. Karma moved his head around to her left ear and whispered sweet nothings. Suddenly, she pulled back for a kiss that caught them both in a passion as intense as it was intoxicating.

"Not in the car." Sakshi's eyes lit up as she opened the door and pulled Karma with her on the cold hard ground.

The grass around was damp. As they made love, Sakshi could see Karma's face glistening with sweat and pleasure, the leaves above and the sky almost midnight blue, and the moon a milky crescent. Their breaths rose in visible puffs and though it was cold, they kept each other warm. "I love you," Sakshi whispered.

"I love you a lot." Karma smiled, caressing her face.

Away from the eyes of people, a love story had fully blossomed in the hills of Darjeeling. The next morning, Karma came to see Sakshi off when she left the hotel.

"See you, baby," she told him.

"Do you not want me to see you off?"

"No goodbyes, Karma. I hate them. I'll see you soon!" Sakshi laughed.

Ah, that laugh. Could it be kissed too? Karma thought. He couldn't help but love everything about her.

1985

Arnab had called for the priest from the nearest temple and had a *puja* and other rituals conducted in the house.

"Why are all the doors and windows closed in the house?" The priest asked calmly and opened one of the windows in the living room, letting fresh air diffuse the scent of the burning sage.

"Ghosts or spirits—whatever you might want to call them—are attracted to negative feelings. I've done what was needed. See, I'm not an exorcist who can cleanse your house. If the activities continue after this, we will have to consult an expert. There is one I know. He is a psychic and keeps travelling for work. Let me know and I'll check with him," the priest informed them and took their leave.

"Does this feel better?" Arnab asked Anuradha, trying to understand if there was a change in their surroundings now after all the elaborate rituals.

"I don't know yet. But there is a lot of smoke for sure." Anuradha smiled and hugged him.

Ricky was in school. They didn't want to scare him more. They were concerned for him. He had been through a lot since they moved to Darjeeling. Everything seemed fine during the day, and when Ricky was back in the afternoon, Anuradha assured him that it would all be okay now.

"How do you know, maa?" Ricky asked his mother while she made him his favourite chocolate milkshake.

"Magic! Don't you know your papa is a magician?" She smiled at him. She felt better too.

"Good! Can I watch a movie tonight then?"

"Which one?"

"I don't know. Anything."

"I'll call your father's office and ask him to visit the videocassette library. It's been a while since we all watched a movie, no?"

She called Arnab. "Ah, why watch at home? Let me pick you two up in some time. Let's watch a movie at Capital, walk to the Mall, buy a few books from the bookstore and have dinner at Glenary's? Sounds good?"

"Perfect!" Anuradha smiled. She too needed some time out and was glad her husband understood it. "Let's take you out for a movie..." Anuradha kissed her son's cheeks as they proceeded to get ready for the outing—their first in Darjeeling together.

1985

The grille design of the front porch entrance of Capital welcomed the three as did the smell of fresh popcorn, uniquely different with its pungent mustard flavour. The crackle of fresh local potato chips and the waft of smoke and mint in the air accompanied them as they watched the movie, a Hindi commercial potboiler. After the show was over, they walked up the Chauk Bazaar to the Mall, located on top of a road, a nice flat land where tourists and localites lounged to enjoy the cool breeze, take a seat on one of the many benches along the periphery and watch the wonderful views of the mountain peaks and valleys all around.

They could see a few Ambassadors, that most luxurious of vehicles, around them. The lucky few who owned Maruti Omnis and Maruti 800s, preferred to sit in the comfort of their cars. It was, however, the Land Rovers that ruled the roads.

Arnab had bought a white Ambassador as he needed to travel daily to the town and required it for his family too. He had parked the car in the market area and decided to enjoy the leisurely walk to the Mall with his family while relishing some ice cream. Everything finally seemed normal. Ricky was carefree and happy that day, just like children are supposed to be. They bought books, rented videocassettes, had dinner at Glenary's and reached home late at night.

"Thanks for the day, sweetheart. It was much needed!" Anuradha hugged Arnab.

"I'm glad things are okay now, darling." He hugged her back. They switched off the lights and cuddled up to sleep.

The next morning, Anuradha woke up early and felt light, like a weight had been lifted off her shoulders.

This day is a lovely new beginning, she thought and smiled. She looked at Arnab who was still in deep sleep. She decided not to disturb him and Ricky as it was a weekend. While Arnab had been dealing with a lot lately, with his new business still in its nascent stage and not much flow of money, Ricky was yet to adjust to his new surroundings, the new school, people, and friends. The unnatural occurrences in the house were over and she knew they could make it work now.

"I will cook something nice for the boys today! But first, let me clean the dingy basement!" she told herself.

The basement was once a wine cellar Arnab was informed by the previous owner of the house.

"That's the only dirty part of the house. Tell me, does the place seem like it is close to a hundred years old?" he had boasted while handing Arnab the keys.

"Spick and span!" He had laughed and left. He was based in London though and had never lived in this house. The most exclusive vintages of Scotland and Europe used to be shelved in wooden racks in the basement, trusted to the natural refrigeration by the soil behind the dense stone walls. There were ancient brackets for candles every few feet, covered in cobwebs. It was musty and dark with a single bulb providing whatever dim light it could. Constructed from quarry rock, its walls were thicker than a medieval castle.

Anuradha walked down the creaky stairs and switched on the light. It flickered and then lit, but still dim for the place to be properly visible. She began cleaning the basement, but it was too dirty and dingy for her to clean all alone, and she realised it would be a futile attempt. Anuradha sighed as she decided to make a move upstairs.

Just then she thought she saw someone walking there. Suddenly, she felt the air around her constricting and a sense of heavy discomfort fell upon her.

She was alarmed. *This doesn't feel good. This feels like...* She knew this feeling. She had felt it before in the house.

"Is anyone here?" she whispered.

"Can you hear me?"

She mustered up all her courage and raised her voice. "This is our house...Do you hear me? Our house!" She did not know who she was speaking to, but a part of her—the protective wife and mother—wanted to assert her power against whatever was trying to disrupt the peace of her family.

Goosebumps rose on her body as if a sudden gust of cold wind had struck her. At first, she could hear the faint sound of someone breathing. Her heart was pounding, and before she could say anything more, she heard footsteps. Its sound kept increasing each second. Someone was running towards her. She screamed and ran up the stairs stumbling and scared. Just as she closed the door behind her there was a loud thud from behind it.

"Arnab..." she called for her husband and was about to rush to his room when someone banged on the door of the basement from the other side. "Who..." Anuradha couldn't control her tears as she stood there frozen with fear.

"Arnab..." she wailed over the increasing noise of the banging.

"Arnab..." she screamed as her husband came running towards her.

"Check on Ricky..." Anuradha shrieked.

"Ricky..." they both called for him.

They could hear footsteps that overlapped with the sound of a lady weeping, as if mimicking the cries of Anuradha, and people conversing. The noises grew so loud that Arnab and Anuradha couldn't hear each other speak. And the door to the basement opened with a loud thump and all went quiet.

Arnab hugged Anuradha, trying to console himself as well as his wife. "The priest was right. We will need an expert. I'll get in touch with the psychic..."

Arnab had taken the number from the priest and called him directly that afternoon. "Yes?" Kirtiman answered the phone.

"Mr Tamang, this is Arnab. Arnab Dutta."

Arnab explained to him all that had been transpiring in the house.

"May I know your address?"

"Glen Manor..."

"I see..." Kirtiman's reaction was quick. "Is there still a large antique mirror in your house?" he asked.

"Yes. There is. Why?"

"I can't say till I visit your house and check but... But you know that mirrors are a portal to the other world, right?"

"The other world?"

"I call it that. There is a world that runs parallel to ours. That is where ghosts and spirits continue to exist in the afterlife. Mr Dutta, that mirror has a history," he told him. Arnab listened to Kirtiman Tamang, too afraid to ask questions he wasn't ready to hear the answers to.

All Karma and Sakshi could remember were the strange things that had happened to them in the house. Their concept of time was altered; they did not know how long they had been trapped inside it. But they did remember the day it had all begun...

That morning, Karma woke up with a jolt. His eyes took in every ray of light and he understood he had slept too long. He observed that it was a misty cold morning and got out of his bed.

"Sakshi..." he called for his wife but there was no answer. "Sakshi..." he called again.

Karma looked for her in every room, on the terrace, every nook and corner of the house but she was nowhere to be found. He only heard his voice echoing in the empty house.

"Where could she have gone?" He was frustrated and decided to go out and look for her, but when he tried to open the main door it didn't budge.

Could she have gone outside to get something and locked me? Karma wondered.

"Damn! This is crazy." He sighed.

"Karma..." It was Sakshi's voice and it came from behind him.

"Sakshi..." He turned back to look at her. She looked pale and scared.

"When did you come?" she asked him.

"What? What exactly do you mean? I couldn't find you and was looking around. Your absence scared me. And why do you look so pale? Come here, baby..." Karma hugged her. Sakshi hugged him back.

"I guess… I had a terrible dream, Karma. I was all… all alone in this house and had been looking for you too. And the door was stuck and not opening..." Her voice trembled.

"It's still not opening… see!" Karma said.

"It wasn't a dream then…"

"How can this be? Is someone playing a prank on us?"

"There is no way someone could steal the key and lock us inside. Why would someone even do that?" Sakshi shrieked.

"Calm down, Sakshi." Karma couldn't see her distraught. "Look at us… we are together, right? We're here and nothing wrong has happened to us. It's all okay. We will figure things out. Come, I'll make you a cup of piping-hot tea. God knows I need one too!" Karma smiled.

CHAPTER FOUR

which meant they had to do a lot of shopping. It took them a few days but soon they setup their house—the start to the life they were excited to spend together.

Sakshi enrolled in a master's course in the same institute where Karma taught—Mount Hermon. But her field was different and Karma wasn't her teacher. Though many knew it, they maintained their distance on the college premises and never addressed the relationship. While Karma decided he would be more open about it after their marriage, Sakshi didn't want the details of her personal life to affect her studies. Karma still made it a point to daily wait for her outside on a by-lane near Mount Hermon. On days when Sakshi got free before Karma, she waited for him at the same place. But unlike before, they rarely went out for dinner and headed home directly. On some evenings when they weren't in the mood to cook, they relied on takeaways. That's how the first few months went by for them and they loved every moment of it. They had a lot of time to give to each other and to get to know each other better. Everything required in a healthy loving relationship, they had it all.

"We are too good to be true," Sakshi told Karma, on the night they celebrated their six-month anniversary.

"Don't ever change. Please. I don't want to lose you." Karma caressed her.

"I won't."

"And when will we get married?" Karma asked.

"Come on, Karma. It's too soon for marriage."

Sakshi never admitted it to anyone but she knew that marriage wasn't for her. She had seen a terrible one at her home and her troubled childhood had convinced her that the idea of a happy marriage was simply a lie. But she also understood that at his age Karma wanted stability, and despite this looming cause of conflict between them, she had faith that their love would be able to overcome all obstacles. *We'll cross that bridge when we come to it*, she often said to ease herself.

1985

It wasn't before evening that Kirtiman Tamang reached the house and was greeted by Arnab at the door.

"Hello, Mr Tamang. Please come in." Arnab tried hard to smile.

"My team, Salil and Tshering," Kirtiman introduced the man and the lady who had accompanied him for the investigation.

"Oh, I thought you worked alone."

"I do. I do. But I also keep travelling these days and Salil and Tshering visit places here when I'm not around. You are lucky I was in the city when you called." He smiled as they walked into the house.

"I didn't know there were paranormal investigators in our country," Arnab informed Kirtiman.

"There are. There are a handful of us right now. There is one in Calcutta too. Chitin Barman. Wonderful fellow. I met him when we were working on a case together."

"Hmm..."

"I get it. You haven't heard of him. Not your fault. Heard about Ed and Lorraine Warren?"

"No."

"They're paranormal investigators in the US."

Arnab nodded distractedly.

"You wouldn't know of them either, of course. Our field of work isn't well acknowledged. Perhaps if someone wrote a book about it or made a movie, we would be known better." Kirtiman chuckled and looked around.

"Do you feel anything here?" Arnab asked, observing Kirtiman while he kept his bag on the sofa.

"Strangely, no. When can I meet your wife and son?" he asked.

"Right now, of course," Arnab said before he called for his wife.

"Just a couple of things I needed to discuss before the session."

"Session?"

"Yes. A séance."

"Is that…"

"Yes, it is. It is required."

Anuradha greeted the three strangers as she walked into the living room.

"Ricky is fast asleep," she informed Arnab.

"How is he now?"

"He isn't feeling well."

"I'm sorry, Mr Tamang. Our son is recovering from flu," Arnab said.

"He falls sick often, does he?" Kirtiman looked curious.

The couple didn't answer the question but the look on their faces said it all. They realised Mr Tamang had a point and their son was falling sick more often now than he did when they were in Calcutta.

"Oh, come on. That proves nothing. It could be the weather too." Kirtiman laughed.

"So, let me give you an insight into the process. Okay?" He was suddenly serious.

"And… you two, please, listen to me carefully. When I'm not around, perform the séances exactly like

I do," he addressed Salil and Tshering, who nodded and smiled.

"The process of paranormal investigation is different abroad. They're quite methodical with it, I would say. They have various instruments at their disposal. We don't have that here. There are no local or national dealers. Importing them would be very expensive. I am sure you can guess that paranormal investigators earn peanuts here. Our clients only ever sponsor our travel and we don't get paid beyond it for our investigations. What we do does not help us earn a livelihood," he said and shrugged his shoulders.

"Look at sir getting sentimental. You can't drive away ghosts by whining, sir." Salil attempted to make light of the matter. While everyone shared a laugh, Arnab flinched at his casual mention of ghosts.

"This is how it should be." Kirtiman looked at him.

"What?"

"Keep it light." He smiled. "Feel at ease, Mr Dutta."

"How can we?"

"Remember one thing. The unwanted energies here were once like you and me. They too breathed. There is always some reason as to why they try hard to latch on to this world.

"My approach to finding the unknown is to start by feeling calm; to acknowledge your fear but not let it overwhelm you. The more you react, the more they react," he informed them.

"So, what's the process like?" Anuradha asked.

"There is a mirror in this house..."

"All houses have mirrors, no?" Tshering asked meekly.

"Poor attempt at a joke, Tshering. Did you know mirrors are portals to theother world, where spirits and demons reside?" Kirtiman asked Arnab and Anuradha.

"We do now," Arnab said. He had trouble taking Kirtiman seriously.

"There is one large antique mirror here in this house..."

"Yes, it is placed in the bedroom."

"That is where we will conduct the séance."

"How... How do you know about this mirror?" Arnab was curious.

"A few people here in the hills know about it. That mirror has a history, Mr and Mrs Dutta." Kirtiman looked at them seriously.

"It's a very old story here in Darjeeling. My grandparents told me when I was little. There lived a man here who claimed he could see the future. His origin isn't known to us but he was a distant relative of the owner of the house and resided here as a caretaker. We also don't know how he died. Some say he conducted certain rituals using the mirror as a medium and ended his life in the process of one such ritual, his last. Others say it was due to a natural cause. However, they did find his body near the mirror. Most people dismissed his story as just another false lore. But what we can't dismiss is that it is a mirror and like I told you..."

"Mirrors are a portal to the other world," Arnab repeated.

"Yes. And so it is an important part of the séance. Can you take me to the room?" Kirtiman asked.

He didn't let it show, but Kirtiman Tamang had felt unsettled the moment he had stepped inside the quaint old house. The air was colder inside. Arnab who had greeted him at the door had a negative energy around him. His eyes reflected the same fear the house seemed to possess; of being isolated and abandoned. Kirtiman could sense these things. He had also discerned the same energy attaching itself to Anuradha the moment she walked into the room. The energy was dark but Kirtiman wasn't sure yet if its intentions were malevolent. Regardless, there was a history to uncover. Something very bad had happened in the house. Kirtiman decided he wouldn't let them know about it till he had with him all the answers.

Karma woke up with a jolt. The wind was knocked out of him, his heart was pounding. It seemed that sleeping too, along with living in the house, had become a dangerous sport. He wasn't sure what he had dreamt but he was with Sakshi, they were meeting each other and holding hands and in the next second they were separated. Karma searched for her in the college where all the students were dressed as clowns. They stared at Karma and giggled. Karma looked lost and confused, still trying to look for Sakshi but she was nowhere to be found. In another moment, they were all gone and everything had gone dark. That's when he woke up.

Karma's eyes flickered in the unlit room. No daylight. *Ah, the storm outside,* he thought. Karma closed his eyes again, hoping to tumble back into his dreams, but he couldn't. Then he heard a loud noise, this time forcing him out of bed. Sakshi was fast asleep. He decided to make his way to the living room to check the source of the sound. The door to the basement was at the far end of the living room. The noise grew louder as Karma walked towards it. The noise, a cacophony of laughs, groans and whispers, reverberated through the walls, its origin shrouded in mystery.

Karma reached the door and opened it slowly. He walked down the stairs and stopped midway to peek into the area—a dingy basement which smelt of damp wood. Originally a wine cellar, Karma and Sakshi used it as a storeroom and would hardly ever go there.

He looked around and saw nobody in the basement but just as he was about to leave, he realised something. The dim bulb which dangled from the ceiling was lit. *How could that be*? Karma scratched his head. Nobody had been there for the longest time. *This isn't possible*. Karma walked to the end of the stairs and looked around. Just then, the noise echoed in his ears first, before reverberating around the room, as if he was the very source of this disturbance. The air around him tightened. The hair on the back of his neck stood on end. Someone was around.

"Who… Who is here?" he managed to stutter. "…Our house!" He heard a woman shriek while hurried footsteps shuffled around him. Everything told Karma to run out of there but his body stood frozen. The next moment, the sound of the footsteps resounded from the stairs… and in seconds the door slammed shut with a thud. At the same moment the dim bulb dangling there exploded, leaving Karma in pitch darkness in which he saw dark red as if he was blinded from his eyes being gouged out. His body washed cold. He brought his fingers to his eye sockets. They were still there. He sighed. Grappling with the darkness, Karma unsteadily walked to reach the stairs. Somehow he managed to stumble to the door and tried to open it but found it locked from the outside!

"Damn!" he screamed and banged the door.

"Let me out!" He kicked it over and over again but it wouldn't open! He was sure he would lose his mind if he was trapped there for another minute.

"Open the fucking door! Open the fucking door!" he screamed at the top of his voice.

It was only after some time that Sakshi heard him and rushed to let out a very terrified Karma from the dingy basement.

"We have to do something..." Sakshi told him, pouring him a glass of water, while Karma sat beside her, looking worried.

"Do what, Sakshi? This storm has to recede first so that we can go out." Karma held her hands and felt better.

"We should... we should call on the entities present in this house..." Sakshi looked at Karma, her eyes revealing more fear than she could allow her words.

"Are you crazy?"

"This is the only way we can be safe, Karma. We both know there is something sinister around here, chasing us. It won't be long before this game ends with us being harmed. We need to communicate with them. We need to find out what they want. We need to tell them that this is our house."

"We cannot venture out in this territory, Sakshi. We are not experts."

"No one is coming to our rescue, Karma. Don't you see? We don't remember when was the last time things were normal, when there wasn't a storm outside, when this house felt safe." Her voice was trembling and desperate. "Come on, Karma. You know about the supernatural. If anyone can do this, it's you. You know how to call on them, don't you?"

"There are ways but none of them are safe, Sakshi."

"Anything is better than being trapped here. We need to put an end to this nightmare."

"Are you sure about this?" He looked at her solemnly.

"Yes, Karma." She hugged him tightly. "We won't let go of each other and of our dream to build a life in this house. We'll save everything," she said firmly, despite her fears.

CHAPTER FIVE

2016

Almost a year into their relationship, the real trials of love came for Karma and Sakshi. The cracks in their dynamic were beginning to show. Over time, Karma and Sakshi realised it wasn't going to be easy for them to be together, despite how much they loved each other. They wanted different things in life. While Karma was looking for quiet stability, something that he hoped his romantic relationship would aid in, Sakshi, young and spirited, wanted her life to be full of excitement. And these differences, which they had dismissed as minor components of their life together, increasingly came to clash in their routine life.

"Let's go out!" Sakshi exclaimed one evening as they left the college. "The night is still young, my friend." She nudged Karma.

"This is Darjeeling, sweetheart. The whole town goes to sleep before the clock hits 9."

"Then, let's go for a drive somewhere!"

"Where can we drive to that's better than our home? I'll cook you dinner and we can watch a movie. Come on, let's go home."

"Ah, you're so boring!" Sakshi sulked and the two went home together. This was a routine occurrence and even though she tried to ignore it, she was beginning to grow unhappy with how Karma always behaved. Silly quarrels and harmless arguments became part of their daily life and soon began shaping into a void in their relationship. And Karma's reticence played into it. His idea of love was different; his preferred way of conveying his feelings was without having to say much.

"Where is the thoughtful guy, who was big on gestures? Remember how you brought me here early morning to propose, Karma? Now I have to beg you to take me anywhere," she often complained.

"Come on, Sakshi. You can't expect that of me always. Did you think the honeymoon phase of our relationship was going to last forever..." Karma would defend himself, annoyed by her criticisms.

"Why not?" she would always ask, unsure why things couldn't be like they used to.

Sakshi often left Karma alone on weekends to go out with her friends while he stayed home trying to get ahead with his writing. Sometimes they would go on for days without properly speaking to each other.

On certain occasions, they pretended to feel normal and put on smiling faces to make each other feel comfortable. These were mostly around friends and the get-togethers they would often be invited to. While they tried to keep their relationship as private as they could, people still talked. Some admired them for the big step they had taken. Others had no faith in their relationship; they dismissed the couple as two impulsive people who had made a mistake they would regret in hindsight. Despite their early devotion to each other and their relationship, Karma and Sakshi felt they were right; they could feel the ghost of regret looming large in their lives. Perhaps they should have given more time to understand each other before plunging into a commitment. And while they weren't married or bound by anything; they still didn't want to walk out of the relationship. Was it because they loved each other? Neither could answer the question honestly; they no longer knew. Matters of the heart are complex as such, but one thing was for sure—things had begun to fall apart in their lives.

1985

"I insist on a small party. Only then will we start our work." Kirtiman Tamang smiled. The voguish middle-aged man knew his job well and believed in making his clients as comfortable as possible.

"You think this is a time for celebration? While you hint that something fearful lurks about in my house."Anuradha looked at him questioningly.

"Why not? You can't stop living because of your fears, Anuradha-ji. That's what spirits feed on." Anuradha looked at Arnab who nodded at her.

"Spirits were once humans too. As I tell all my clients it is important to extend your empathy to the dead. Whoever is terrorising your house is unhappy. And to find out why, you have to first accept that the spirit is here for a reason," he said. "Besides, never let anything come in the way of good food and drinks, not even spirits!"

"It's okay, Anuradha. I'll get the drinks, you bring the food."

Anuradha went to the kitchen while Arnab offered the party some drinks and observed the three men. "Aside from the thing about the mirror, we have no other information about this house. But something tells me there is a lot more here… That mirror can't be the only cause of trouble..." Kirtiman said and began instructing Salil and Tshering about the procedure they would be following. Arnab couldn't understand a word of it especially since they decided to discuss the details in whispers. He could however make out that Salil and

Tshering were amateurs and respected Mr Tamang a lot for his work. There was genuine sincerity in the way the three of them planned the way forward. He could see that Mr Tamang was a thorough professional with a defining quality—he was an empathetic man.

"You know what I believe? I'm a doctor." There was a mischievous twinkle in Kirtiman's eyes as he spoke while they all sat together in the living room. Anuradha brought them platefuls of finger foods and crispy *samosas*.

"Don't you call for a doctor to cure your physical ailments? And here you're consulting a paranormal investigator… a psychic… a ghost doctor, call me what you will, to cure the haunting and the haunted. My job is pretty simple to understand that way," Kirtiman concluded.

Anuradha smiled. "I suppose we are in good hands." She understood why Mr Kirtiman Tamang was considered an institution in himself when it came to parapsychology.

"Now let's get to work." Kirtiman looked at his protégés and they proceeded towards the room where the mirror was placed.

"And what do we do?" Arnab asked.

"You can stay with us and enjoy the show. Just don't get scared!" Kirtiman laughed as they made a move towards the room. "Let the doctor find out more about what ails this house."

Salil and Tshering walked closer to the mirror to have a good look at it.

"Oh, come on. We're not playing Bloody Mary!" he told them. "We will sit a little far from it… here…" Kirtiman indicated the place.

"Sir, I was just checking!" Tshering giggled as the three took their positions a few steps away from the mirror and sat facing it in a half circle. Arnab and Anuradha sat watching them from the bed.

"Do we start with the ritual?" Salil asked.

"No, Salil. We don't use any techniques that remotely resemble religious practices. Just my psychic abilities should help."

"But there must be a process...?"

"Many of my earlier studies revolved around the Mayans and their beliefs about reflective surfaces. They believed mirrors and even water surfaces were portals to the other world where not just where the spirits dwelt but also other godly beings. As per them, portals were connections between multiple worlds and allowed active engagement between the Mayas and their gods. The Maya practised many rituals, from bloodletting to using substances, to possibly experience a higher state of being. The underlying purpose of those rituals was to achieve some form of communion with the gods, whether seeking their favour or simply scrying. Portals were a way to that communion. The same was true for communicating with spirits. There are still ways that make this process more complex but I prefer to stick to simply one thing—establishing a two-way contact. Wherever there is a haunting, there is always some reason behind it. They want to communicate as much as you want to. We need the right intent to summon them and they will respond. Now trust me, and follow my lead," he said and asked them to maintain absolute silence so he could focus.

Nobody said a word while Kirtiman meditated. About half an hour later, Arnab began to lose his patience.

"Mr Tamang... nothing is happening..." he whispered.

"Shhh..." Tshering asked him to remain quiet.

Kirtiman opened his eyes and looked at the mirror. There was nothing amiss in the reflection.

"This is unusual. I should see some disturbance in the reflection by now but..." He stood up to answer him.

"There is something here that doesn't want to communicate with me..."

"What do you mean, Mr Tamang? You are the psychic here. How would we..."

"This only means one thing..."

"What do you mean—" Arnab's question was interrupted by the echo of fast-approaching footsteps.

The sound rang loudly around the house like the racing heartbeat of a condemned prisoner. It came to a halt and the door opened...

"Ricky..." Anuradha called out.

"Shhh..." Kirtiman cut her short. This was the first time he seemed nervous. "The mirror is not our medium." He looked at Ricky and in a hushed voice said, "He is."

Ricky entered the room and stood in front of the mirror. The room was filled with absolute silence once again.

"A little boy… a woman…" Sakshi mumbled to herself.

"What?" Karma asked.

"Karma, is it possible that our visit to that haunted place invited something bad in our house? What if it followed us here that night?"

"Which night… Oh, come on! It was nothing. We were just having some fun."

"Think, Karma. Our relationship has not been the same since. Things have been going haywire! And now we are here… trapped in this house…"

"The headless body of Dow Hill and the weeping lady..." Karma pondered over the urban legend attached to that place and tried hard to recall if anything had happened the night he took Sakshi to visit the haunted place.

"This stretch here between the Dow Hill Road and the Forest office is called the 'death road' and that's the forest area... there..." Karma pointed in the direction of the forest, leaning on the bonnet of his car while Sakshi sat on it.

"There, as per the lore, roams a headless boy. People have reportedly seen him walk around and disappear into that forest..." Sakshi finished his story. "'A Few True Urban Legends' is the best book you have written so far. I've read it twice," she said.

"I thought I could have written it better though..." Karma admitted.

"Of course. The self-critical writer." Sakshi laughed.

"Now tell me, do we get to see the ghost of the headless boy today?" Sakshi asked.

"If we do, we'd at least know the stories are true. There's no definite proof that he exists. Many locals prefer to call them rumours because such things affect tourism," Karma spoke like an expert.

"Let's check out other haunted locations then? Where do you take me next? Margaret's Hope?"

"You will find many such ghost stories in the tea estates. They've been here since the British era. In a way they carry memories of all that has happened in the past..." Karma said thoughtfully while driving on a narrow stretch of road leading to their next destination.

"Chapter Five from the same book." Sakshi smiled.

"Damn. Why do I feel like I'm taking you on a tour based on my books?" Karma smiled too.

"Well, you're doing a decent job of being a guide," Sakshi teased him as she looked out of the open window.

After driving for another half hour, Karma stopped the car. Here too there was complete silence and not a single person in sight.

"So are we going to find out if the spirit of Margaret is a rumour too? No chance of seeing her tonight?" Sakshi looked at Karma.

Karma turned off the ignition and the headlights of the car died out. The car was engulfed in pitch darkness. Outside they could see little golden dots blinking. The fireflies were too few to attract Sakshi's attention.

"What are you doing, Karma? Turn the lights on!" Sakshi held Karma's hand tightly.

"Scared?"

"No, I'm not!"

"Oh yes, yes, you are! Admit it!" Karma teased.

"Stop joking around, Karma."

"First say it... you feel scared!"

"Karma!"

"Sakshi!"

"Okay... okay. I'm scared ... only slightly!"

Karma turned on the headlights and laughed lightly. "This fear is a new look on you! I'm sorry, we'll leave now. Let's go have dinner at your favourite restaurant."

"Nothing happened that night, Sakshi," Karma confirmed.

"What if you are wrong Karma? We have to communicate with them to find out," Sakshi demanded.

Karma paused and sat down for a few minutes. Deep down, he knew Sakshi was right. This was the only way out.

"There are various ways to summon the dead..." Karma opened a book he had written and turned to the page, handing over the book to Sakshi to read. "This is the one we need."

"A portal?" She looked afraid.

"We'll need a mirror. They are portals to the other world. This particular process involves long winding steps and various kinds of rituals. I wrote the precise steps in this book after researching with and interviewing paranormal experts. We will keep it simple though."

"So, we'll just have to meditate and concentrate on the mirror?"

"Well, yes. But we aren't psychics so we'd have to change things a bit. Let's follow this..."

Karma prepared a Ouija board using a large piece of paper, covering it with letters of the alphabet, the numbers 0 to 9, and the words 'Yes', 'No', 'Hello' and 'Goodbye'. Once it was ready, they lit candles in the room, which emitted a crepuscular glow, and waited for some wax to collect, after which Karma sprinkled it on the mirror with some salt. Once it dried, the two of them sat facing the mirror and placed the Ouija they had prepared on a small table in between them.

"If there is anyone here with us, manifest yourselves. We summon you here!" Karma looked around. Silence hung heavy in the air, poisonous in its nothingness. It grew eerie as the seconds passed by. Karma and Sakshi were unnerved by it, a gaping vacuum that seemed to be closing around them slowly.

"Is there anyone here? Show yourself!" Sakshi tried to impale the silence with her sharp voice. It was followed by the pattering rain that began to pour again outside. Those drops were bigger than prairie hailstones and coming down just as hard. They played drums with the windows, cymbals with the concrete floor and soft maracas with the grass—music that was only sad and scary for Karma and Sakshi.

"I don't think it's working," Sakshi whispered.

"Let's keep trying. This is the safest and easiest way to call them."

"Maybe we are doing it wrong?"

"Is there anyone? Show yourself." Karma raised his voice. Sakshi and his fingers were placed on the upturned glass on the Ouija board. They looked like little children playing a made-up game in the dark. Fifteen minutes passed but nothing happened. The rain too had stopped.

"Do you hear it too?" Sakshi looked at Karma nervously. Karma strained his ears to listen.

The noise came from the outside. "I think... it's coming from the living room," Karma answered.

"We should go and check..." She held his hands as they stood up to leave the room. The noise they were following suddenly stopped as they inched closer to the living room. "There's nothing here, Sakshi. We should go back and keep trying."

"Then where was that sound coming from?" And just then it was heard again; this time a lot clearer—a loud clinking of glasses. There was no one in the living room but they felt like they were walking into a gathering of a few people who were merrily chatting.

Terrified, Karma and Sakshi looked at each other. And then, they heard the piano. Someone was playfully pressing its keys.

"What is going on, Karma?" Sakshi looked at him. "Were we successful in calling the spirits? Is this part of the process?"

"Where is Ricky?" rang a man's voice.

"In the other room. He is asleep," a woman answered, and they heard the creak of a door. The next moment, someone walked into the room Karma and Sakshi had been in. Its door opened and shut by itself.

"This is getting crazy…" Karma cried.

"And we'll fix it, Karma. I need you to stay strong. We have to call on the spirits." Sakshi hugged him as the noises intensified around them and suddenly stopped. They went back and sat in front of the mirror and placing their fingers on the upturned glass, they summoned the entities together.

"If there is anyone here with us, show yourself!"

"If there is anyone here with us, show yourself!"

Each time they said it, their voices got more confident.

"If anyone is here with us show yourself!" they repeated together.

Then they heard it. A loud crack.

Karma and Sakshi looked at the mirror in front of them in sheer terror as it started to crack in the middle, distorting their reflection. All the windows in the house were shut yet a gust of wind swept into the room and blew off the candles.

CHAPTER SIX

Crack.

Karma and Sakshi looked at it in sheer terror as the small crack now stretched across the mirror.

"You don't belong here. This is our house," Karma and Sakshi said together.

A few seconds later, the planchette moved. A faint voice called them towards the broken mirror. They looked at it and saw an apparition getting closer to the surface. It was icy white and wispy, as if a cloud was materialising into a body. Within a few seconds, there was an outline of a face and a body; but it was still not fully formed. The apparition seemed to be taking different shapes.

Sakshi turned to Karma. "The spirit has responded," she whispered. "Perhaps, it has something to tell us." Fear engulfed them as they sat there in the dark room. What were they to do? *Will we have to make the first move?* he thought.

The cracked reflection now contained a fiery red, translucent object scintillating a hazy green glow. It took some time before it took a clear shape, like an object far away slowly coming into focus. This ghoul was close, very close!

At first, its whisper was like the soft susurration of the wind in the trees; then as its silhouette became sharper and his face clearer, the whisper became an eerie rasping voice, moaning and groaning.

"No," it said.

The voice was like iron nails dragged over a rock. It rose and fell, uttering unclear words. Then the eyes that had been gleaming red turned to black and the mouth stretched wide in a scream so loud that the glass windows pulsated with its echoes.

CHAPTER SEVEN

2018

There were days when Karma didn't feel like going home after his lectures. He always had the evening free to do as he liked, and before Sakshi had become part of his life, he would spend his time working on his books. It was only now that he didn't know what to do with himself. He hated going home and was too distracted to focus on writing. Thoughts about Sakshi disturbed him. His life had become limiting; his entire world revolved around Sakshi and now that his insecurities infiltrated their relationship, he had nothing left to be happy about. Karma and Sakshi hardly met in college, especially since it helped maintain their relationship a secret, but despite their attempts, rumours and gossip were rife on the campus. Most people spoke in whispers about the couple and had many theories about their relationship. This was also the time when Sakshi was seen spending all her time in college with Tenzing, and it wasn't long before people were raising their eyebrows at their growing friendship. "Have Sakshi and Karma sir called it quits and is she dating Tenzing now?" "Is she two-timing Karma sir?" "Do Karma sir and Sakshi share an open relationship?" were some of the questions that made the rounds. Sakshi was aware of what people talked behind her back but she did not want to dignify their crass ideas with explanations. She felt secure in herself and, regardless of the problems in her relationship, had faith in Karma's love for her. Little did she expect that what she had dismissed as harmless rumours were going to turn sinister and ruin her completely.

There was a dingy hotel in the town infamous for being a favourite spot of young couples. Word spread that Tenzing and Sakshi were seen entering that hotel together in the evening. The source of this rumour wasn't known, and there was one woman who knew how to use that to her benefit. It was time for a third person's envy to put the final nail in the coffin of Sakshi and Karma's deeply strained relationship.

A professor at the college, Vaishali, had known Karma as long as he had been on the campus. In fact, Karma, socially awkward as he was, had found Vaishali's company enjoyable. However, while Karma had found in her only a good friend, Vaishali had fallen for him. She had given several hints to Karma, in the hopes that he would reciprocate her feelings, but clueless as ever, he had continued to keep her at a distance. And when she had lost her patience and grown tired of waiting for him to understand her feelings, Vaishali had decided to confess her love. Had Karma let down her proposal kindly, perhaps she wouldn't have done what she did, and perhaps it would have saved him and Sakshi. But on hearing Vaishali's feelings, Karma had apologised to her and decided not to speak to her as he used to. He felt a constraint in their friendship and didn't want to confront it to seek a resolution.

So, when Vaishali heard of the gossip surrounding Sakshi and Tenzing, she knew she had found a way to get back at Karma for the way he had treated her. After all, he deserved to know of the foul things his partner was found doing, she thought, and decided to put her plan into action. That day, Karma had just two lectures in the first half and instead of going home he ate a quiet lunch alone and sat in his cabin, just to be by himself. There was work to finish but he was too miserable to tend to it.

"Can I come in?" Vaishali had knocked at his door.

"Yes, please." Karma sat up straight.

"Are you free for a quick chat?"

"Oh, yes. It's one of those days when I only have two classes."

"Ah..."

"Is there something important?"

"Yes. Actually." Vaishali knew it was time to strike.

"Sure. Please have a seat."

"I don't know how to tell you this... Karma..."

Karma was not in the mood to entertain her but tried to convey it politely. "The suspense is of no use, Vaishali. Whatever it is you can tell me," Karma said.

"It's not easy for me to... but I thought I should. It's regarding something I heard about Sakshi..."

Karma wasn't listening to her but that got his attention.

"Hmm?"

"I don't know what you'll make of this, but I thought it'd be wrong if I didn't tell you."

"Vaishali, will you come to the point, please?"

"Well, Sakshi was spotted with Tenzing in Hotel Annapurna."

"What?"

"I thought I should let you know before you found out from someone else…"

"There must be some misunderstanding." Karma's voice was hardly audible as he spoke to himself. *This can't be true.*

"I hope it is a misunderstanding, Karma. But the entire college is talking about it. You know how news spreads here, right?"

She glanced at him and observed the expression on his face change to that of worry.

Karma's eyes were moist. "I think you should leave now, Vaishali. I want to be alone."

"I'm always here, always a call away when you need me. Take care, Karma," Vaishali said before leaving.

Karma sat there in his empty cabin wondering if it could be right. His head was spinning. Was their relationship really at this stage now? *Am I being cheated on,* his mind kept repeating as his rage built up and took over and there was no rational thought left in his mind. He cried in anger. He was so lonely. He had nobody with him. What had his life come to? And he hated himself for it. He trusted Sakshi but he knew he had always been insecure. He was aware of Sakshi and Tenzing's growing friendship and tried to console himself that she would never betray his trust. *Had he been foolish in his faith?*

Karma couldn't think straight and he wanted to let everything go. His desperation led him to the nearest bar in the town. He wasn't a teetotaller but he never drank excessively. But that night he cared for nothing.

It was 10 p.m. when Karma stepped out of the dingy bar. The guy at the valet parking brought his car and handed him the key.

"Maybe you should call someone to drive you, sir." The valet looked at his state and suggested he call someone to drive him home.

"You don't tell me what I should do," he shouted at the valet as he got inside his car and drove away.

1985

"Whatever is going on here is not because of my séance alone. There is surely some other force at play. Your son has cracked the channel of communication with the spirits in this house…" Kirtiman Tamang told Arnab and Anuradha.

Ricky's astral body was stuck in the other world where he could see a man and a woman. He knew their faces; he had seen them a few times in the house. He had always been afraid of them, but now they looked terrified. He had seen the man in the living room more than once—sometimes pacing the room in circles as if in a trance, sometimes walking up to him when he played the piano. Sometimes he saw him playing it instead. He had seen the woman too, but his connection was stronger to the man.

Ricky had always seen them around the house. They had terrorised him for the longest time. Stuck in this confused state, he could not only see them but also hear them clearly.

"This is our house…" they kept saying.

"Please leave…" they begged.

"No," Ricky whispered.

"Please…"

"No!" He raised his voice. He was angry. "It is our house," Ricky said.

The wind howled outside, rattling the ancient windows. And in the room, they heard the panicked screams of a man and a woman. Arnab and Kirtiman exchanged nervous glances. The lights flickered. Once, twice, and then went out, plunging them all into darkness. The only illumination came from their flashlights, casting eerie shadows on the walls. They heard it again—a scream, blood-curdling and desperate. It was the scream of a man, followed by a woman's anguished cry. The sounds came from everywhere and nowhere, echoing through the corridors. The air was cold. The screams grew louder, more insistent, as if whatever was trapped there wanted them to partake in its suffering.

"The energies from the two separate worlds have finally come to clash," a worried Kirtiman said under his breath.

The apparition vanished seconds after Karma and Sakshi saw it in the mirror, leaving them in the dark room. They could feel a heavy presence of some energy around them. They had succeeded in establishing a connection with the other world. Now they needed to know why the spirit was haunting their house so they could figure out a way to drive it away.

The room lit with the flashes of lightning just when the planchette moved, slowly at first, then with more force. It spelt out a message for them: LEAVE.

"Who are you?" Karma shouted.

The couple's fingers followed the planchette as it spelt a name Karma hadn't heard in ages:

R… I… C…K… Y…

Scared, Karma moved his hand away, and the planchette jerked violently, flying off the board and skittering across the floor.

CHAPTER EIGHT

2018

When Karma reached home late at night, he saw Sakshi waiting for him outside on the veranda.

"Where were you? I was so worried! Your phone is switched off. And they said you'd left the campus early. What's going on?"

"Hmm..." Karma tried to walk straight on his feet but was dead drunk.

"Kar... Karma... Are you drunk?"

"I'll go and freshen up... Let's talk during dinner," he said, patting her back and then left. Half an hour later, Karma came out of the bedroom slightly sobered and looking fresh.

"What were you doing out drinking this late at night, Karma?" Sakshi was losing her patience with him.

"Who are you to ask me these questions? Are you the only one who is allowed to indulge yourself? Look at what you have been doing..." Karma said to her sharply.

"Yes?" Sakshi had been serving dinner. She kept the utensils on the table and walked up to Karma who sat on the sofa.

Karma looked up at her.

"And what have I been doing?" Sakshi was angry.

It was either the alcohol or his confused emotions but Karma laughed and stood up to face her.

"What? Why are you looking at me like this?" Karma asked.

"What is wrong with you?" Sakshi asked, trying to keep her calm.

"Everything! My life is wrong… This so-called relationship is wrong," Karma screamed at her.

"Why carry on with it then? Do you want to end this? Fine then, I'll leave tomorrow." Sakshi kept her ground but didn't scream at Karma.

Her composure irked him even more. "Of course. Isn't this what you were waiting for?" Karma stepped closer to her and held her tightly by the shoulders.

"You are hurting me, Karma." Sakshi raised her voice.

"Look at what you have turned me into, Sakshi. Just look at me. I was perfectly fine before you entered my life. How I wish we hadn't met…" Karma let her go and took a step back. He felt ashamed of himself.

"Do you… Do you feel nothing for me?" Karma sat down on the floor with a thud.

"What are you saying, Karma? Where is this coming from?" Sakshi tried to let go of her anger and console him.

"I'm… I'm going crazy and it's all because of you!" He punched the floor hard.

"I know things haven't been okay between us…"

"Us? Where does 'us' figure in this relationship? It's always you; your fun, your life, your decisions…"

"Listen to yourself, Karma. Am I all to blame? Have you ever made any attempt to adjust to my needs?

"But you fell in love with this guy only, no? You fell for me after knowing me…"

"I can tell you the same thing, Karma… I left my family for you…" she cried.

"Oh please! Not this cliché again! And what is this family you talk about? You very well know about them…"

"Karma, I'm warning you…"

"I've had enough of you…"

"I've had enough too!"

"Fine then…" Karma went quiet for a few seconds. Then he asked her quietly, "Will you tell me the truth?"

"What truth?"

Karma was spent and wanted an end to his misery. "The truth about your relationship with Tenzing."

"We are friends, Karma. How can you doubt me? Do you not know me at all?"

"I have my reasons, Sakshi. I know you and that swine went together to Hotel Annapurna. That's where young couples go and fuck, don't they?"

Sakshi looked stunned.

"I didn't think you could stoop so low..."

Sakshi rushed to her room and began packing her bags.

"So what, you will walk away because you don't have an answer?" Karma followed her to the room.

"You're willing to believe a bunch of rumours against my word? Gossip dies when it reaches a wise man's ears. Unfortunately, you are a fool, Karma."

"Sakshi… listen to me…"

Karma's heart shattered into a million pieces as he watched Sakshi pack her bags. Perhaps he had let his insecurities get the better of him, he thought and repented.

Sakshi excused herself and walked to the living room. Karma followed her and pleaded. "Tell me the truth, Sakshi," he asked calmly.

"No, I won't. You have already made a judgement yourself..." Sakshi looked into his eyes sternly.

"Everyone on the campus is saying..."

"And you believe them but not me?"

Sakshi held Karma's hands. Karma's eyes were flooded with tears.

"Just tell me the truth! Please..." he screamed and pushed her away.

1985

Ricky's astral body knew no fear. As his physical body stood still facing the mirror, his soul connected with the spirits in the house in the other world. Kirtiman, his colleagues, Arnab and Anuradha could hear voices in the room.

"Please leave our house…" The man and woman seemed to plead.

"This house may have been yours. But it belongs to us now," Ricky told them. The man and woman seemed to get closer to him. He was coming from a world of light and entering a world where there was none, barring the short flashes of lightning.

Ricky could see them now. They looked distressed and confused. He stared at them as they came closer to the mirror. They could see him too.

The man looked shocked. His mouth fell open, sheer disbelief washing over his face. "How can this be? How can this be?" he heard him say repeatedly.

R… I… C…K… Y…The planchette spelt and Karma leapt back in fear.

"Do you know anyone by that name, Karma?" Sakshi asked him.

"My parents...they used to call me Ricky…" Karma could barely speak as his mind dug up suppressed memories.

"Look…" Karma pointed at the mirror.

"Please leave our house…" they said together.

"This house may have been yours. But it belongs to us now." They heard a voice as a little boy appeared in the mirror looking straight into their eyes.

Karma stood up and walked closer to the mirror. He froze at the image he saw. He couldn't believe his eyes. "How can this be? How can this be?"

Karma was in a state of disbelief. What had they done? He was scared to think. A thin veil separated the real and the other world, he knew. The spirits of the other world could be furious beings, wanting to make their presence felt, or desiring to be a part of the physical world to mend the things that went wrong and find resolutions to their regrets. Had they destroyed the divide that kept the two worlds separate? Karma went over all that had happened to them in the house. His face drained of colour, as he pieced together everything he knew and the weight of its realisation settled heavily upon him.

"I think I know what is going on," Karma said and looked at Sakshi.

"Do you remember that morning when we both woke up but couldn't find each other?" Karma held Sakshi's hands, kissed them and looked into her eyes. "It started with a nightmare and we will have to live it until we reincarnate..."

Karma was uncomfortable the entire night. He'd heard a little boy call out to him in his dreams and his voice had snapped him awake. Sakshi was fast asleep next to him. That morning, seeing her sleep peacefully relieved him of all the distress he was feeling about their relationship for so long. He got out of bed and paused to look at himself in the mirror. Karma stared at his reflection as if in a daze when suddenly, a child's apparition, though unclear, appeared and disappeared on the mirror, jolting Karma out of the spell he was under. "Sakshi!" he screamed to wake her up.

Karma kept calling for her but found his voice betraying him. No sound came out of his mouth. The very next moment, he found himself back on the bed, sweating and breathing heavily, and realised he had just woken up from a nightmare. He turned to Sakshi and gently put his hand on her shoulder; she turned to him but it wasn't Sakshi's face but his own looking back at him. Shocked and confused, Karma tightly shut his eyes hoping this was another bad dream.

When he opened his eyes again, he was sitting in front of the mirror again, still yelling Sakshi's name but audible to no one. And then, he woke up with a jolt again.

"Sakshi…" he called for her and walked out of the room to look for her.

"I remember..." Sakshi sobbed.

"That was a new morning in a new world, Sakshi. You woke up before me because you had entered this world before me. Which is why that morning you were alone in this house, and you couldn't find me until I came looking for you. I followed you to the other world, Sakshi," Karma said.

He had finally accepted what he suspected was true all along—they were dead.

CHAPTER NINE

2018

"Tell me, Sak..." Karma froze when he looked back after he had pushed Sakshi.

Life stopped for him. There was absolute stillness around him. His shock blocked the sound of leaves rustling outside; the wind had died for him. He had trouble breathing, his mouth went dry and his eyes refused to blink. Karma walked up to where Sakshi lay in a pool of blood and stared at her face. Minutes passed but he was paralysed from disbelief and couldn't make a move. He could see his blurry reflection in the blood on the floor that was trickling out of her head.

She could be dead, the thought snapped him out of his mental freeze.

"No, no... She'll be okay... She'll be okay..." he repeated to himself and went closer to her body. He touched her face and found her skin growing cold. She wasn't breathing and his fears were confirmed.

"I have killed her," he said under his breath.

Karma looked at the wall where Sakshi had banged her head when he had pushed her. There was a big nail protruding out of the hard stone wall. It was covered in her blood which had also splattered on the wall.

Karma sat there beside his lover's dead body, staring at her. Nothing made sense anymore. He didn't know what to do. He couldn't even cry. He felt settled in this heavy silence and thought he'd stay there for eternity. It was only when his hand fell into the pool of warm blood that his passivity was replaced by action. How could he live without Sakshi? His whole world had crumbled; all he could feel was pain, but even that wasn't enough. He had to do something. He was desperate to punish himself for what he had done.

And then he decided—he wouldn't live without her. That night, Karma hung himself from the ceiling fan in the living room. And even as he felt his last breath slowly slipping out, the pain still didn't compare to the grief he had felt from his actions. It was 1:10 a.m. when Karma too lost his life.

1985

After Ricky's apparition faded from the other world, his physical body came back to life in front of the large mirror in the real world. Everything appeared blurry at first and he felt weak, as if something inside him had been missing for a while. Startled with no memory of what had happened, Ricky looked around and saw his parents, Kirtiman and his two colleagues staring at him. Something was strange indeed. Ricky felt so too. He had no clue why he was in front of the mirror and no memory of how he got there. All he remembered was that he had fallen asleep and in his dreams, he had heard voices calling out to him. The voice of a man and a woman… they wanted to tell him something.

"Ricky, are you okay?" Anuradha rushed and hugged him tightly. Arnab patted his head and asked him if he was hurt anywhere on his body.

Ricky looked at them in amazement, wondering what was wrong. "I am okay. Are you both okay? Did something happen?"

Arnab and Anuradha didn't explain anything to him. They didn't want to burden him with information that could scare him. Kirtiman and his two protégés left their house, content after successfully solving another case.

From that day on, no supernatural occurrence bothered the family during their stay in Darjeeling. They lived a wonderful life the next two years—the memory of which Ricky would forever cherish. Busy with his fun life and the adventures of growing up, it didn't take long for

Ricky to forget the unnatural incidents he had witnessed in the house.

"Maybe, the spirits just needed to communicate," Arnab said to Anuradha one day.

"I am just glad all that is over. This is no longer a haunted house! Just our home away from the madding crowd..." Anuradha smiled. And so, it remained for the next two years until another tragedy struck their family.

Arnab and Anuradha were to go to Siliguri one morning for a meeting. "We will be back at night. Papa has an important meeting and is asking me to accompany him. Tell me, what can I bring for you?" Anuradha cuddled Ricky as he was getting ready for school.

"Hot Wheels!"

Anuradha smiled, nodded and kissed her son's forehead.

"Hey, champ. We will go out for dinner tomorrow, what say?" Arnab held him in the air while Anuradha walked behind them with Ricky's school bag.

"I say yes!" Ricky laughed as his father tickled him.

"I'll drop him at the bus stop and then come to pick you up, Anu. Then we'll leave!" Arnab walked out of the house with Ricky.

That morning was the last time Ricky saw his parents. They met with an accident on their way back to Darjeeling and were declared dead on arrival by the hospital. Ricky was eight years old. Arnab's father took him away from Darjeeling and the house he had known as his home was no more.

"I'll come back," Ricky promised to himself as he left Darjeeling sitting in the back of his grandfather's car.

The Other World

"This storm is never going to stop. And we know why," Karma spoke to Sakshi and looked outside the window, realising what he saw was not the real world. Karma Dutta, aka Ricky, had moved into the Darjeeling house with his parents in 1985 and within a few days had a frightening premonition after which he began to experience strange things in the house. The supposed paranormal events had lasted for a month when a paranormal investigator was called to help, referred by a priest who had earlier paid a visit to the house. He conducted a séance of which Ricky had little recollection and suddenly everything was back to normal for him—until two years later, when he had lost his parents. He grew up with his grandfather in Calcutta, only to return to Darjeeling and the house that was his home.

Apart from the realisation that it was Sakshi and he who were haunting the house after death, Karma also understood that he had been haunting himself as a child. The strange unexplainable occurrences in his childhood were due to his own spirit trying to communicate to his younger self. *There is no concept of time here, we're stuck in an endless space,* Karma realised. Everything he had studied and researched about when he was alive turned out to be true.

"We exist in a dimension where everything is contained in a single moment, we can touch any point in the past and present while the real world moves on following its rules of time. It all stopped suddenly... or so I thought back then in childhood, Sakshi. There was a reason why it all stopped... I am that reason..."

Karma turned towards Sakshi who sat on one corner of the bed in the room.

"We must accept the truth. Maybe then I'll stop haunting my childhood. This storm will never pass. It will never let us go anywhere else." Karma went up to Sakshi and kissed her hands to console her.

"We could have dealt better with things, Karma. I could have been more understanding; you could have been less insecure. I wish we had tried a little harder to make it work." Sakshi sobbed.

"I wish we had, too," Karma said calmly. "We can only accept what is our truth now. We will be at peace if we try not to latch on to the physical world."

Sakshi nodded and hugged him.

EPILOGUE

The soft, warm morning sun gave way to a new day. Driving in the sunshine, the warm blacktop led onward into the horizon, taking a loving family to their new home.

"Beautiful, isn't it? What were we even doing all these years?" The man driving the car looked behind and smiled at his wife and two children sitting in the back.

"I'm giving you my word, sir. You will love it here," another man who sat beside him spoke. He paused for a minute and then continued, "Just that..."

"Just what?"

"I told you, sir. The house has a history," the broker said.

"Oh, you mean about its last owners?"

"Yes," the broker spoke in a hushed tone.

"In that case, every house or apartment has a history. That doesn't mean all of them are haunted, does it? Besides, we don't believe in these things. Don't worry."

The man stopped in front of a big old house. The family got out of the car.

"Our new house!" the children said in unison and ran to the main gate, where a board read 'SOLD'.

The broker smiled meekly and handed the keys to the man who opened the gate. The family entered the house together.

Karma and Sakshi were stuck in the dark and gloomy house while a storm roared outside. They could not leave until they were allowed entrance to the spirit realm and, depending on their karmic pattern, a chance to reincarnate.

Suddenly, they could hear the voice of a man, a woman and some children.

New residents had come to live in their house. They looked at each other. "I don't like this disturbance," Sakshi looked wickedly at Karma who winked at her.

In the living room, one of the chairs was pushed back and its noise grabbed the family's attention. They stopped talking and looked around. "It's nothing. Must have been a rat or something…" the man said. "Come, let's check out the piano," he suggested to the children to divert their attention.

His wife looked around the room hesitantly. There were no signs of rats.

"Don't worry. It was nothing," the man said to her to allay her concerns. "Surely, you don't believe what the broker said," he said and laughed nervously. "Surely, there are no ghosts in this house."

ACKNOWLEDGEMENTS

I have always believed that gratitude is the best attitude, and like all my other books, *Karma* wouldn't have seen the light of the day without the support of those who have played a part in its journey, both directly and indirectly. It is said that writing is a solitary process but getting the book out is the combined effort of many people.

First and foremost, I thank my literary agent, Suhail Mathur of The Book Bakers, for having faith in my craft and representing me. Your guidance and suggestions have been invaluable to me. I'm also thankful to The Book Bakers for designing the striking cover of this book.

Thank you to the entire team at Om Books International for bringing this book to life. Thank you, publisher, Ajay Mago; editor-in-chief, Shantanu Ray Chaudhuri; and my editor, Chakrika.

With sincere gratitude, I would also like to thank my parents, Chandrani and other family members who have understood how different I am and been accepting of it. Thanks for bearing with me!

Dear Kaira, here's hoping you will enjoy this book too when you grow up and read it. You inspire me with your angelic smile. Love you to the moon and back!

Thank you to my readers and reviewers. I earnestly hope you will have a good time reading *Karma* and show it all your love (and fear!), as you have done so for my earlier books. There is a lot more to come and I hope you are as excited as I am! Here's to our 'Karmas'.

Read well!